BENT OVER TO PLEASE

DIRTY BILLIONAIRE BOSS

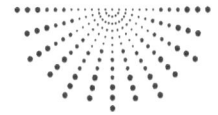

TALA MELTON

plicit Press
Erotica Fiction

GET NAUGHTY UPDATES

Click here or Visit
TalaMelton.com
for more Naughty Maid Stories

eISBN: 978-1-62327-702-4

Print ISBN: 978-1-62327-703-1

CHAPTER ONE

"What do you think of this one," middle-aged billionaire Damon asked his young house-keeper. Alexa was anxious about turning around because Damon had the habit of asking her to help him choose a shirt... in his underwear!

She turned to find the *too sexy for his age* billionaire standing in the kitchen, completely naked except for a shirt. The shirt was a pale blue, with diagonal detail in the same blue, but for a good minute, this shirt was the last thing Alexa was thinking of.

"It's nice," she said after she managed to remove her eyes from the generous *sausage two eggs breakfast* between Damon's legs.

"It's okay, really. I've always been a nudist. But if it makes you uncomfortable, then I'll *try* when I'm around you... I really just needed advice about the shirt... I really hate these things!"

His explanation made sense, of course. Damon was used to living alone. So he was used to doing things a certain way... His way. And if he was a nudist, then he was a nudist.

Alexa remembered him mentioning something of the sort during her interview. She just assumed that this meant he liked to *swim naked?*

"I think I'll wear the other one," Damon said, breaking the silence. He turned around and walked up the stairs, Alexa's eyes on his beautiful butt. It really was an incredible *behind*, and Alexa was grateful that Damon didn't have eyes in the back of his head.

When he came down the stairs for the third time that morning, he was fully clothed. He looked a little more put together than he usually did, even shaving. Alexa wasn't sure which look she liked better, all of them suited him. His nudity suited him.

She poured him his coffee as he sat down for breakfast. He opened up the first of three newspapers in front of him, already perfectly placed.

"Are you happy here?" he asked when she placed the coffee in front of him.

"Very..." she said.

"It isn't too much work for you?"

"Not at all..."

"Good!"

She served him his breakfast without mention of his penis. Alexa appreciated this because Damon usually *toyed* with her discomfort. She really didn't mind, though; it was just unusual. When he left her alone in the apartment, she closed and locked the door, went to the kitchen, and started doing what she was paid to.

It really wasn't too much work. Cleaning after Damon was easy because he was so neat. Alone now, she thought of her billionaire boss. He really was attractive, and he knew it. And he really liked being naked.

She did wonder, sometimes, if it was an attempt to entice and seduce her, an experienced play for her innocence. She was a little naive, so she had no idea how to read flirtation. *Was this flirtation?*

The doorbell rang loudly, and this irritated Alexa. Daydreaming about Damon was *her* time, her guilty pleasure, and now it had been disturbed.

The sound of the bell, again, fused now with the sound of the street down below, really was very intrusive. Usually, every sound disappeared into the background, but once you heard them, you couldn't unhear them.

"Delivery for Mr. Damon..." the *not unattractive* delivery guy started.

"Yes, I'll sign for it!" Alexa interrupted.

She closed the door and put the package on the desk in the hall so that it was the first thing he saw when he got in. Then she went to finish up in the kitchen before making her way upstairs to go through Damon's wardrobe. He was going to be away on business for a few days and needed her to pack for him. *Formal* was a dress style he didn't understand, and so having Alexa choose his clothing for the series of meetings he would be attending was the safest.

After making his bed, she lay out the various options. He would have three *out of town* meetings over three days, so she coordinated the outfits in sets of three. His *in-between* looks were his worry.

Trousers and shirts matched a jacket in a contrasting shade for each option. Socks and belts a basic but bold black. No ties!

If this maid gig didn't work out, Alexa could really have a career as a stylist.

She hated it, though, *picking* clothing she couldn't afford, *trying* on clothing she couldn't afford. She never went window shopping for just this reason.

It was easy for her to do it for Damon, though. Firstly, it was sort of her job. And secondly, that a billionaire trusted her with how he presented himself to the world was really a deep compliment. When she was satisfied, she cleaned the rest of the room before moving on to the rest of the apartment, which she would give a thorough cleaning over the next couple of days when she was alone!

CHAPTER TWO

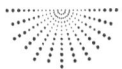

*I*t was already past 8 when Damon returned to find Alexa putting his dinner in the oven. If he arrived early, he usually found her still there, and she did the few things he had neither the desire or often the ability to do himself.

A quarter after 8 was early!

He walked into the kitchen carrying the package from the hallway. "You're still here," he asked - *always the same question* - as he opened it. She didn't answer, taking his dinner back out of the oven instead.

"Must I bring your dinner upstairs when you're done in the shower," she asked, referring to the fact that he was incredibly sweaty still, and he was still dressed like he'd only just run off the squash court. He even still had the racket in his hand.

"I suppose I must get clean... You can bring my dinner up in the meantime, and a drink... A double vodka over three rocks. I should be done before the ice melts!"

Damon leaped up the stairs, not unlike a child might have, skipping two, sometimes four whole stairs. Alexa watched this, not because she enjoyed him *leaping over tall buildings in a single bound*, but because he wasn't wearing any underwear, and his purple-headed python was peeping out the bottom of his shorts. Even clothed, Damon still managed to make you look!

She still watched the stairs long after he had disappeared out of sight.

Alexa put the warm plate on a tray, took it upstairs. Damon was already under the shower, the outline of his perfect frame visible almost too clearly through the frosted glass. She put the tray down on the table near the window and went back downstairs to fix the drink. By the time she brought it upstairs, Damon was drying himself rigorously, moving the towel from side to side across his back.

She didn't apologize for the first time. Alexa just walked to where the dinner tray was set up and placed the glass neatly next to it. She turned to face Damon, who had at this point, dropped the towel on the ground and was standing in front of the outfits laid out on his bed.

"I like all of them," he said, lifting one of the jackets.

"You should; they are your clothes..." Alexa answered, a little too familiar, so she dropped her head.

"They're mine, but I didn't buy them. Your predecessor did!" He obviously hadn't noticed her cheeky remark, or he just didn't care.

He was still picking up and putting down items of clothing. His back to her, he turned just his head to face her. "You're going to the same soon; once I've been seen in these once or twice!"

"Surely you don't care what people say about how you look," she asked, again bordering on *too familiar.*

"I don't...but the world does. And the least we can do is give them a show worth watching, don't you think?"

"I suppose," she said, after explaining the best order in

which the options worked. And when it was clear that Damon wasn't going to put clothes on, she asked if she could leave.

"Just a minute, if you don't mind. I want to try out the ones I really like, and just get them packed once and for all. I'm leaving at 5 in the morning, and it will just go quicker with a little help?"

"Sure," she said, as she stepped forward, closer to Damon after grabbing his suitcase from the closet.

She stood behind him as he picked up a shirt and put it on. He turned to face her as he buttoned up before sitting on the bed to put socks on. Then he was standing again, pulling trousers up to his long, muscled legs, and finished up quickly with the belt. After slipping on his shoes, he walked over to the mirror to see himself, followed by Alexa, who was carrying one of the jacket options.

She helped him into the jacket, which perfectly completed the look. Damon looked more impressed then he was before, Alexa, too, was very happy with herself.

"Yes..." she said, smiling broadly.

"One down," said Damon, already out of the jacket and taking off the trousers carefully, handing them to Alexa. She took them, her eyes between her boss's legs, for just a moment. He saw her look, and this made him smile. There was a slight sexual tension in the room now, probably the hour, probably the fact that Damon was naked again. Fortunately, he was already pulling the second pair of trousers up his legs.

Back in front of the mirror, he was as impressed with this second look. He took it off quicker and handed the items to Alexa to be packed away. Then he walked naked to the table and finished his drink in one gulp. He sat down, asked her to get him another drink, and started to eat his dinner before it got too cold to enjoy.

He was finishing up by the time Alexa returned with his drink. She placed it on the table in front of him, went for the tray.

"No, leave it..." He was looking at her, through her.

"One to go," she said, needing to change the subject. Although what exactly the *subject* was, wasn't exactly clear.

"Are you in a hurry," he asked, making her even more nervous by the way he asked.

"Not at all..."

She really just wanted to be away from him now. Her uniform was suddenly very hot, and she just needed to get out of it. Alexa was a woman, she was a young woman, and Damon was a very attractive man. But she couldn't, she knew, be with him naked like this, and resist the urge to touch him.

Is that what he wanted, she wondered again. If it was, then why didn't he just make a move? Why did he not just take her, stake a claim on her as he did with companies daily? She wouldn't resist, wouldn't say no. Surely he knew this.

Her eyes were on his semi-erection. His eyes were on the top button of her uniform, where just enough flesh was showing to let him know that she had ample breasts. He was walking towards her; she was unable to move. He stood in front of her, towered over her, and put his hands on her shoulders, saying suddenly, "I really want you..."

"Then take me..." She really needed him to.

CHAPTER THREE

*D*amon bent down, kissed her on her neck, swelling his erection to full. It was red and veiny, the purple head looking like the stuff of dreams, or nightmares, depending on your penchant for kink. He unbuttoned her uniform and let it drop to the ground. She was wearing panties, *no bra*.

Damon got on his knees in front of her, and he pulled her panties off her. He held her, hands-on-hips, and pulled her close to him so that he could inhale the scent of her where her thighs met. She almost fell over, holding herself up by holding on to his head with both hands.

"I've wanted to taste you for weeks..." His confession came just before his tongue made direct contact with the outside of her. There was no need for Alexa to make any confessions of her own, because she was getting what she'd also secretly wanted for weeks now, too. It was the ultimate win-win.

Damon's hands dug into her waist, his fingers pressing hard into the flesh until they made contact with her hipbone. He pulled her into himself harder, into his face, his mouth, and he was literally *eating her out.* In fact, he was putting the *eating* in that phrase.

Alexa forgot, momentarily, that Damon was her boss. She was grinding into his mouth, feeding him all of her he could safely consume with each bite, each lick, each nibble. He hadn't forgotten the nature of their relationship, though, so that when he summoned the strength to pull away, he looked up and asked her, "Are you sure?"

Her response in the affirmative was clear. She grabbed his head and put his mouth back where it just was. What on earth made him think he would get off the hook now that he had her hook, line *and proverbial* sinker?

He enjoyed his *meal* for the longest time so that Alexa began to worry that this was all he was going to do to her. Surely he had more in his arsenal than just the best cunnilingus she had ever had.

For the moment, though, it was clear that this was all he wanted. His eyes were closed, and he was lost to the world. Alexa wondered if he just really enjoyed the act, or if he really enjoyed it with her. She needed it to be the latter, of course, since it had only been done to her twice before - *but never like this* - and both times, she was showered with compliments.

When he finally pulled his face from her, she'd had three maybe more orgasms. They weren't mild by any stretch of the imagination, but Alexa had always been an *internal cummer*. She orgasmed, right enough, but to the sounds of clashing cymbals inside her head, inside herself.

Damon had worked on her so long as a result of this, in fact. He wasn't sure he was giving her any pleasure, and so he just carried on, unaware that he was, in fact, delivering multiple orgasms to the silent sweeper. Her legs shook now, threatened to buckle underneath her so that Damon came up to standing and lifted her off the ground. He carried her to the bed, lay her down, and finished his drink.

Then he was back, next to her on his back. He held her hand on his shaft, moved it up and down slowly, an effort to get her comfortable with the size. Nothing he did now or ever could get her comfortable with what looked, at a glance, like 12 inches.

He left her to move her own fingers up and down on him now. He watched her, delicate fingers, neatly clipped nails, shiver and shake her way up and down his shaft. He looked at her face; she was looking at his meat.

"We won't do anything you're not comfortable with..." He spoke into the room.

She tried her head for an answer, *thank you* seeming a little inappropriate and expected. So she just firmed her grip on him and moved her hand up and down more determined.

He leaned to the drawer on the side of his bed, took out a tube of lube, and with her hands still on him, squeezed a generous amount of the strawberry smelling gel onto himself. This definitely made it easier for her hands, and also, it meant that if this handjob was all he was going to get than at least it was going to be a good one.

Damon lay at a diagonal on the bed now, and with Alexa's hands still moving up and then all the way down on him, fingertips on his balls, he reached down and pulled her legs so that, quickly and unexpectedly, she flipped all the way back so that her thighs straddled his face. He didn't even need to lift his head, just pulling her down a bit so that she was in his mouth for the second time tonight.

Alexa rubbed Damon's head across her lips. He shuddered at the unexpected sensation. Then her mouth was over his head, working down the lube-covered meat with ease, stopping not a centimeter short of the base.

"What the Fuuuu...' he mouthed. He actually said it, quite loud, not expecting this at all.

Alexa had always seemed shy and inexperienced. That's what informed his approach when he knew he wanted to sleep with her. And just moments earlier, her hands were shaking, something he assumed was because of the incredible apprehension she felt at having to *take all of him.*

And then this happened. Practically every inch of him had disappeared into her mouth, which must have a secret compartment because where else could he have gone. He lifted her off his face completely so that he could get visual confirmation of what he felt had just happened.

It was just so!

Alexa moved her mouth up to his head, and then back down, settling him so deep in her mouth so that just his nuts were not swallowed. He was breathless, still in complete disbelief as her mouth moved the full length of him, both ways, without skipping a beat. She had decided on the rhythm and pace, and she was sticking quite comfortably to the speed limit.

After *forever*, he pulled her so that they were face to face. He tried to articulate how impressed he was but couldn't find the words. He pulled her to him and kissed her harder than before. His eyes were opened and on her, not wanting to risk that this was a dream, and she would be gone when he opened his eyes.

He watched her closely, as she worked her way back to his throbbing parts with her mouth. It was no less veiny. It was no less menacing. But she knew that looks were always deceiving when it came to penises. What you saw was certainly not always what you got, a lot of it resting with the man attached to the meat.

"You are the reason..." he said when again her mouth was off him and they were face to face.

"The reason," she asked.
"The reason kings have given up kingdoms!"

CHAPTER FOUR

*H*e had Alexa on her back now. Her body glistened in the light of the room, the beads of sweat clearly visible on the surface. She was watching him carefully, anticipating his next move. Her body tensed slightly at the thought that, at any moment now, he might mount her. She tensed even more, when he was just tracing up and down the full length of her body with just the tip of his index finger.

This finger commanded meetings, she knew. It commanded men, spurred them on to great achievements designed, at their core, to increase Damon's Dollars and Dividends. It was a very powerful finger.

It landed on her, rubbed slow circles into her *flower*, which bloomed magnificently, more than she had ever seen it bloom before. Her body certainly didn't respond this way when she touched herself. It had certainly never reacted as willingly with the other *count them on one hand* men she had been intimate with.

"You're very responsive," he said, watching closely the

space between her thighs, the pink blossom quivering at his touch.

She wanted to say it was just him. She wanted to let him know that he was the best she had ever had. She wanted to word all the truths that would boost his ego and make him more eager to please her, but she didn't. So she just lay back, her eyes on his finger, her mouth open to allow the release of the softest purrs.

She really was purring...

Then the finger on her became two, the circles more determined. He tapped her lips, not quite a tap, not quite a smack. Then again, he was tracing the slowest circles around the outside of where he was pulling just the slightest trickle of goo, her reserves still somewhat depleted from the multiple orgasms of earlier.

Alexa bent her knees, only to have her legs straightened again by Damon's free hand. She struggled, the natural response to being pleased this way had always, for her at least, been bending the knee. He wanted her to feel something, clearly. He wanted to control her in a way that let her know that he was controlling her, that he and only he was giving her this pleasure.

It wasn't even an ego thing. Damon had no ego, not in the traditional sense. He had a quiet arrogance borne of incredible achievements. Many, many achievements, in fact. So, this was him, in his natural element. He was doing what he needed, what he wanted, in a way that made the other person more open to doing whatever he wanted, later.

His middle finger slipped into her, all the way. She wrapped her legs around his hand and kept this finger from moving. So tight was the wrap, though, that she rendered his hand incapable of any movement now.

Damon let her have this moment. If she needed a minute, a minute is what she would have. He just watched her now, slithering over his hand, his finger deep inside her. He traced the outline of her body with his free fingertips, causing her to shudder and shake just that much more.

Then his hand was out of the death grip, his finger free of her depths. He watched her a moment longer before he brought his mouth to hers. They were kissing each other now, the moment perfect.

Damon put both hands under Alexa, lifted her off the bed, and onto himself. Her legs wrapped around his waist, both of them sitting upright now on the bed. They were still kissing like they had kissed each other in a million previous lives.

The truth was, Alexa was just an amazing kisser. So was Damon. And the two of their mouths together just made magic.

It was Alexa who, seeing the clock on the wall behind them, seeing it was a quarter shy of midnight, initiated the next move. She straddled Damon comfortably and as comfortably eased his veiny warrior into herself. There was no time to play now, not if she was going to pull everything she could from this night.

"Where did you come from," he asked as he settled deep inside her.

She didn't answer him. Alexa just pushed him down onto his back and proceeded to ride him beautifully. She was determined that he would have an orgasm before she left the room, determined to be the only memory of home he had over the next three days.

She moved on him like a skilled rider on a stallion. Backward and forward, back and all the way *forth*. She pulled him almost away from himself with just the muscles of her thighs, the many muscles forming her internal feminine folds. She rode him back and forth for the longest time, bringing him close to climax but not quite. Then she was dancing wide circles of pleasure into him, again bringing him close but not close enough. Over and over, she tried and failed to draw an orgasm from the power tool inside her.

"I need to..." he started, and then went quiet, again so close he could see it.

"You need to..." Alexa started, and then she was caught in her own unexpected climax, Damon holding her in place and driving himself into her from below.

There was nothing she could do about it. She had focused so much on Damon *cumming* that she had neglected her own body's response to the 12 solid inches hitting every part of her. She looked at him, half apologetically.

"Don't worry about it," he said, easing her down from her reverie by moving her ever so slightly in every direction on his still-hard self.

She held tightly onto him, her legs still wrapped around him, still connected to Damon where it mattered. Damon, very carefully, lay her down so that her head was at the foot of the bed, and he was on top and still inside of her. He wasn't moving. Every part of him wanted to thrust into her hard, to drive himself home, but the look on Alexa's face said that she had bitten off more than she could chew.

Damon pulled out of her slowly. It was so slow in fact that just as his head was left inside her, he dug into her completely one more time before pulling out a little quicker this time. Then he left her to recover and went downstairs to fix himself and her a drink. Alexa was spent, really exhausted, but still determined to pull at least one orgasm from Damon. She checked the clock. It said a quarter after two. Dammit, she thought. He would probably come upstairs and ask her to leave so that he could get at least a few hours of sleep.

"Are you still okay," he asked when he appeared with the drinks.

"I'm perfect!"

CHAPTER FIVE

*H*e handed her her drink, and she sat up to take it. Then he sipped his own, bent down and kissed her, and then set about packing the rest of his *away* items in his suitcase. She watched him move through the space, like he owned the whole world. He probably owned a large chunk of it, she thought.

Damon was watching her from the corner of his eye. He was watching her watching him, liking that she thought he didn't see her watching him. She really was nothing like he'd expected her to be. But this was in every one of the best ways possible. He was not disappointed. And he hoped that she wasn't disappointed either.

Alexa's eyes fell regularly on Damon's still-hard *D*. He really needed to cum. He really wanted to cum, but the gentleman in him couldn't bring himself to ask a still-tired looking Alexa for *assistance*. He resigned himself to some in the shower *DIY* in a bit, but then, as soon as he was done packing, as soon as he was done closing the zipper on his suitcase, he turned to come face to face with Alexa.

It was actually more his penis to her face, because she was

on her knees, her mouth already opening to receive him. He watched himself slide into her mouth. He was impressed by the view he had now of this achievement that had so surprised and impressed him earlier. He watched as a skilled Alexa worked her mouth on every part of him for as long as it took him to drip almost uncontrollably with precum.

Watching her work on him was beautiful. He could have done it for hours. He didn't have hours, though, and so he lifted her off the floor and took her to the bed. Again she was shaking, shuddering at the thought of being taken by him. When she had initiated it earlier, there was some semblance that she was in charge of. Now, she sensed, he needed full control if he was going to have the orgasm that she was determined he have.

He lay her down on the bed, his mouth on hers, his finger slipping deep inside her. When they were comfortably on the bed, he added a second finger and did not move. Then, slowly, carefully, he tried for three fingers. The stretch was incredible, the fit tight, but slowly, three of Damon's thick fingers were inside her.

She did not move. He did not move, not his hand, at least. He pushed her higher up on the bed, his fingers still deep inside her. Alexa couldn't think, trying in vain to process the invasion on her nether regions. Then, one by one, the fingers were out of her, and Damon was positioned on top of her, replacing his fingers with his *firepole*.

His thrusting wasn't urgent, despite the hour. Damon just drove himself into her over and over again, watching her closely. Then, he pulled out completely, and again the three fingers, one at a time, were inside her. He played this game of tag for a while. He seemed to be enjoying her responses to him so that the time didn't matter. It was getting dangerously close to 4 AM though, so they both knew that either way, this needed to come to some sort of a head, soon.

Damon knew that there was one way that would assure him of an orgasm. He looked at Alexa again as again he replaced his fingers with his *man meat*, deep inside her, in slow, beautiful strokes. She seemed to be in it now, really in it, but he wondered if he could expect of her what he really really wanted.

He decided that he wouldn't ask. He decided that he would just guide her in the general direction of what he wanted and hope that she did not object to his guidance.

CHAPTER SIX

*A*lexa turned with very little resistance when Damon repositioned her. He had her on her stomach now, still flat on the bed, looking just that much more appetizing in this new position. Damon had just one kink, one fetish. He absolutely loved hitting it from the back. He knew that he was bigger than most, but he absolutely loved being given that other, somewhat *sacred* space.

The other participant had to be willing, though. There was no fun in it if they weren't both enjoying it. He wondered if Alexa would enjoy it. He wondered if she had given it up before and if she liked it. He was wondering a lot of things as he fit himself inside her from the back. Her *punani* quivered on the entry, her walls not resisting him, collapsing instead in on themselves so that his meat was once again for the millionth time caught snuggly in the grip of her womanhood.

He lay on top of her, his chest on her back. He kissed the back of her neck. Then he turned her face so that his mouth fell on hers, and they were once again making magic with their mouths. He drove himself deeper into her in this new position, turning himself on to his side, bring her with him. Damon lifted her leg over his so that he had an uninterrupted view of himself moving in and out of her.

She was also watching his python moving in and out of her. The visuals and the sensation didn't quite sink up. They didn't quite match up. He seemed to be moving in and out of her with an ease that was nothing like the completely delicious destruction that it felt like.

"You really are something else..."

"So are you..." he said, looking back at the clock, seeing that just five minutes had passed. Time seemed, thankfully, to be dragging now. If only it would just standstill. If only!

Damon turned again so that he was once again on Alexa's back. He fed himself into her as he brought her to her knees. She came easily. She really was putty in his hands. And the *sculpture* he intended to build was nothing short of spectacular. He went into her over and over again until she was comfortable on her knees.

He held her hips now, tight, hard, and pulled and pushed her on himself. He wasn't moving. This wasn't necessary. Alexa just dug her hands into the bed, gripped the covers, and let him do with her what he wanted.

Damon was nowhere near getting what he wanted from her, though. What he needed was to be inside her *other* hole, but still, he wasn't sure that she was ready. And she still had no idea what it was he was after. Alexa just expected that at any moment now, he would cum, and that would be that.

It was Damon who was watching the clock now. It had just gone twenty after four. He was cutting it close, he knew, but there was no turning back now. He would see this through to the end, and if push came to push, he would shower on the plane. He started to make all the excuses he needed to make for himself to justify the fact that he was still inside Alexa when he really should have been jumping in the shower.

He pulled himself from her, took the lube in hand, and positioned himself back behind her. Again he was inside her, thrusting steadily, sure of himself. He dropped lube directly on her butt cheeks and as he thrust, massaged the oil into her cheeks towards her hole.

He was feeding himself into her aggressively, now. His fingers found the inside of the hole he wanted to occupy, just two, going as deep as he was in her front. Then a third finger, and he was digging deep. He removed himself from her punani and used his love stick to beat down on her cheeks as his fingers, not so gently, stretched her hole. He couldn't think about her state of readiness now, knowing that, if nothing else, it would all be over very soon.

Damon parted her ass cheeks, dropped an excessive amount of lube in and on the place he wanted now. Then, still holding her cheeks apart, he guided himself into this hole, just his head at first, then the first couple of inches. Then he was all inside her before she had a chance to completely process what was going on. She breathed deep, relaxed as best she could, and received the intruder she did and didn't expect.

"I'm sorry..." He was whispering.

Alexa took another deep breath and pushed back against him so that all of him was inside her. She pulled away, only just, and pushed back against him. She did this a couple of times, convincing him that one, it was okay for him to be doing what he was doing, and b, that she was really very into it!

"Okay, I guess I'm not sorry..." Damon said, grabbing her hips and pushing her towards the headboard at the same time. She grabbed the board, and braced herself, back arched, ass in the air. This was it, she knew. She just needed to brace herself against what would be a full and final assault.

Damon pounded himself into her over and over again. He was home, and it felt good. He had 15, maybe 20 minutes. He only needed 5, he knew, if she didn't move. He hoped that she wouldn't move. He sent himself into her harder and harder, his orgasm rising up to meet him. It was a long time coming, but now that he was there, he felt relieved.

"I'm close," he said, sending several swift strokes deep into Alexa.

She said nothing, just arched her back a little more, fed her ass to him a little more. There was nothing left for him to take. She had given him everything and then some. She had surprised herself with the full summary of *everything*.

He was gone now. The sounds escaping him let her know that he was minutes away. It was seconds in fact, and finally, at last, he was emptying himself into her. He moved hard for two, maybe three more strokes, and then he was done. No movement anymore, not from him, not from her. She collapsed in a heap, half leaning against the headboard. Damon held on to her hips, keeping himself inside her as long as he could.

He brought her down to lying on the bed as he removed himself from her. He kissed her on the back of her neck and the side of her face before leaving her alone on the bed. He got under the shower, with minutes to spare. By the time he was dressed and ready to leave his cab was here.

He watched her a moment longer, and then he absolutely had to leave—everything that he wanted to say to her he could say when he got back. Part of him wished she was going with him. He knew that there were parts of her that warranted further exploration. But it was too late to drag her with him, and her presence could prove a major distraction.

When he left the apartment, it was again deathly quiet. It was so silent in fact that it woke Alexa several times; each time, she just had to remind herself where she was and that it was a safe space, and okay for her to be there.

CHAPTER SEVEN

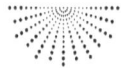

*I*t was almost midday when Alexa finally *woke up* woke up. She knew exactly where she was and how she had gotten there. Still, though, she felt like she should probably get up and get out of there.

Her own room was on the bottom floor near the kitchen. She went to her own bathroom and took a very long shower. She actually wished she'd opted for a bath, but she did need to get Damon's bedroom clean, and she could always bath later.

After she was clean, she stopped in the kitchen to get herself some water. She was a little *tender* but in a very good way. She still felt exhausted, but with a solid reason why, this wasn't altogether unexpected. Alexa was *happy* tired...

Damon called briefly, just to check that they were good, and to make sure she would still be there when he got back.

"Of course, I'll be here," she reassured him. She did wonder, after the call, though, why her predecessor had left. She wondered why all Damon's help had suddenly upped and gone. She was curious, but it was really neither here nor there. Alexa decided there and then that she would not be sent running by what was the best sex she had ever had.

Ever!

She set to cleaning his room. She did, despite her best efforts not to be cliché, do that thing where she stood in the center of the room smelling the sheets. They smelled of her, and him. The sheets smelled of *them*. It was a beautiful smell just because she knew what it was. The traces of strawberry lingering in the air added a touch of the exotic.

Alexa stood in the bedroom for a while; the bed made to perfection. She thought of how many other maids had been in her position, cleaning up the master's bedroom not just after the master, but after herself. She wondered this for the briefest moment, and then her mind went elsewhere.

What use was it to think about who had come before her? She was there now, and it was clear that Damon enjoyed making love to her. She enjoyed being made love to by him. She knew, of course, that there would be other women. This wasn't by any stretch of the imagination any sort of relationship. It was, fundamentally, a very carnal arrangement, one she hoped would last a while still.

There was a lot that could be learned about lovemaking from Damon, she thought. He had years of experience on her, and it seemed he was a willing teacher. Alexa knew that she was definitely a very willing student.

The spring cleaning that she had planned to do over the next couple of days took her just that afternoon. She sat in the kitchen alone to a late dinner, microwaved lasagne and a glass of red wine she knew Damon wouldn't mind her having. Her head was no longer filled with thoughts of her billionaire boss. She was thinking instead of how to pass the time over the next few days, with nothing to do, nobody to look after.

She sipped the wine slowly, ate as slowly, and relaxed into

the stool, thankful that her body was up to the challenge that was Damon. She hoped it would put up with her, bear with her as she explored her sexual limits in the safety of this apartment, where the walls had eyes but did not see, ears that could not hear, and secrets that they would never ever tell.

ABOUT THE AUTHOR

Tala Melton is an emerging erotica author of naughty maids and their billionaire bosses.

Readers: I want to expand a few of the stories to see where the characters can be explored further. If there are any of the stories that you would like to read more about again, I'd love to hear from you!

Visit my blog at Tala Melton Blog
Join my newsletter for free exclusive previews Tala Melton Newsletter
Follow me on Twitter at Tala Melton Twitter
Like my page on Facebook at Tala Melton FB

Sign up for Free Stories from Xplicit Press Authors
Xplicit Press Updates
Like Xplicit Press on Facebook
Follow Xplicit Press on Twitter

MORE NAUGHTY MAID STORIES BY TALA MELTON

Naughty Maids and The Dirty Billionaire Bosses